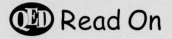

A Cloak for Swallow

First published in the UK in 2005 by
QED Publishing
A Quarto Group company
226 City Road
London EC1V 2TT
www.qed-publishing.co.uk

A Catalogue record for this book is available from the British Library.

ISBN 1 84538 173 4

Written by Anne Faundez
Designed by Zeta Jones
Editor Hannah Ray
Illustrated by Adam Relf

Series Consultant Anne Faundez
Publisher Steve Evans
Creative Director Louise Morley
Editorial Manager Jean Coppendale

Printed and bound in China

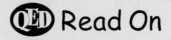
A Cloak for Swallow

Anne Faundez

QED Publishing

QED

Swallow shivered.
He had to fly away.
He should have
left weeks ago
but he'd had
such fun with
his friends.

4

And now snowflakes soft as down
were tumbling from the sky.

"It's too cold here," he cried. "I must leave
early tomorrow. I'll wish my friends
goodbye and then prepare for my journey."

"Owl! I must fly away before the snow sets in," Swallow said.

"Why don't you shelter in your nest until spring?" asked Owl.

"I'll be even colder when my nest turns to ice," replied Swallow.

Owl fell silent.

"Say goodbye to everyone from me," said Swallow. "I'll see you all again next spring."

Owl knew Swallow should have left weeks ago.
The snowstorms would make his journey long
and difficult.

Owl hugged Swallow goodbye.
He was worried about Swallow.
Very worried.

Suddenly, Owl had
an idea, and went
to find his friends.

Owl called a meeting of the birds.
"We must help Swallow," he said.

"How?" said Magpie.

"We could make a
cloak to keep him warm
on his journey," said Owl.

The birds fluttered in excitement.

Just at that moment, Moon was on her way up the sky. She paused and listened to the birds.

"We'll finish by dawn," said Swan, "if we start now."

"We'll have to work all night," said Kingfisher.

So that's what they did.

They gathered some feathers and began to weave them together, in and out, in and out. They worked on and on, weaving and winding.

And Moon shone down and gave them light.

13

Soon, the birds were too tired to go on.
They looked down at the bundle of feathers.

"We still haven't finished and
Swallow leaves tomorrow," wailed Robin.

"We'll finish tomorrow, early, before Swallow leaves," yawned Kingfisher.

So the birds went home, tired and disappointed.

"The birds worked hard," said Moon,
"but there's still lots to do."

She sprinkled moonbeams
and began to weave
them, in and out,
in and out.

She worked until
dawn, weaving
and winding.

16

The birds woke early.

What a surprise!
The cloak was
ready – and
it was shimmering
with silver threads!

Owl smiled up at
Moon as she slipped
down the sky.
"I also wish Swallow
a safe journey," said
Moon softly.

The birds rushed to Swallow's nest.

"Look, Swallow! We've made you a cloak.
And Moon helped, too. Put it on.
It will keep you warm when you
fly," said Owl excitedly.

18

Swallow hugged his friends as the snow began to fall.

"Thank you! I'll see you
next year," he said.

And Swallow set off on his
journey, warm and happy.

What do you think?

Why does Swallow have to leave?

Can you remember the names of Swallow's friends?

Who had the idea
of making a cloak?

Who helped the
birds to make
the cloak?

21

What was the cloak
made from?

How did the birds
make the cloak?

22

What would you like your friends to make you?

What other item of clothing could the friends make to help keep Swallow warm?

Parents' and teachers' notes

- Together, look at the cover of the book and predict what the story may be about.

- Explain to your child that the swallow is migratory, as are many birds. It leaves northern Europe at the beginning of winter and flies to southern Europe and then across to Africa, returning to Europe during the spring.

- Look at a map together to see just how far a swallow journeys.

- Before reading the story, look at the pictures. Can your child piece together a narrative from the visual clues?

- Read the story together, pointing to each word as you do so. Did the story differ from your child's expectations?

- Explain to your child that dialogue in a story is set within quotation marks, or inverted commas, and that each character's speech is set out on a new line.

- Choose lines of dialogue from the story and practise reading with expression. Can your child make up a different voice for each of the characters?

- Encourage your child to paint a winter landscape showing bare trees, snow and blustering winds.

- Can your child tell the story from Moon's point of view? At what point would the story start if Moon was telling it?

- Ask your child to draw a picture of his or her favourite character. Can your child think of an item of clothing that the birds could make for this character?

- Have a go at simple weaving. Collect about a dozen coloured ribbons or long scraps of material. Take six ribbons, place them horizontally and glue the ends to two pieces of card. Now take the remaining ribbons and weave them, one by one, in and out, through the horizontal ribbons.

- Talk about the birds that you might find in your neighbourhood. Can you identify them? Go for a walk and see how many birds you can spot.

- Make up a new story about Swallow. Who might Swallow meet on his travels? What could happen to Swallow next?